MY LIFE AS LOTTA

A House Full of Rabbits

STERLING CHILDREN'S BOOKS
New York

An Imprint of Sterling Publishing Co., Inc.
1166 Avenue of the Americas
New York, NY 10036

Originally published as "Mein Lotta-Leben: Alles voller Kaninchen" by Arena Verlag GmbH written by Alice Pantermüller and illustrated by Daniela Kohl

ISBN 978-1-4549-3624-4

Library of Congress Cataloging-in-Publication Data

Names: Pantermüller, Alice, author. I Kohl, Daniela, 1972- illustrator.
Title: A house full of rabbits / Alice Pantermüller ; illustrated by Daniela Kohl.
Description: New York : Sterling Children's Books, [2019] I Series: My life as Lotta ; book 1 I Audience: Grades 4-6 I Summary: "Lotta has just started middle school-but life isn't going very smoothly. First of all, she has a teacher named Mrs. Crabbert-who is very, well, crabby. Then, her mom gives her a recorder that seems to make mysterious things happen. Lotta also wants to get her own pet . . . no matter what it takes. But her parents' refusal to consider her request, a fight with her best friend, and that weird recorder keep getting in the way. Can Lotta make it all work out?"-- Provided by publisher.
Identifiers: LCCN 2019026158 I ISBN 9781454936244 (hardcover)
Subjects: CYAC: Best friends--Fiction. I Friendship--Fiction. I Family life--Fiction. I Middle schools-- Fiction. I Schools--Fiction. I Humorous stories. I BISAC: JUVENILE FICTION / General I JUVENILE FICTION / Animals / Rabbits
Classification: LCC PZ7.1.P35748 Hou 2019 I DDC [Fic]--dc23
LC record available at https://lccn.loc.gov/2019026158

Distributed in Canada by Sterling Publishing Co., Inc.
c/o Canadian Manda Group, 664 Annette Street
Toronto, Ontario M6S 2C8, Canada
Distributed in the United Kingdom by GMC Distribution Services
Castle Place, 166 High Street, Lewes, East Sussex BN7 1XU, England
Distributed in Australia by NewSouth Books
University of New South Wales, Sydney, NSW 2052, Australia

For information about custom editions, special sales, and premium and corporate purchases, please contact Sterling Special Sales at 800-805-5489 or specialsales@sterlingpublishing.com.

Manufactured in Canada

Lot #:
2 4 6 8 10 9 7 5 3 1

09/19

sterlingpublishing.com

Alice Pantermüller

MY LIFE AS LOTTA
A House Full of Rabbits

Illustrated by Daniela Kohl

For Emma,
who long ago made a down payment of
one dollar for "her book."

FRIDAY, AUGUST 19

Woohoo! Today I started fifth grade!
I don't go to elementary school anymore.
Now I go to the Wilt Whatman Middle School.

I've been looking forward to
this all summer.

Me!

mesh sleeves

I was totally **excited**
and wore my favorite
dress. The one with
the mesh sleeves, like
that mosquito netting
stuff you hang
at the windows.

But **prettier**, of course.

Mom  went to school
with me, because there
was going to be a ceremony
in the school auditorium,
first thing.

Dad couldn't
come with us. He's
a teacher himself
and had to go to
his school.

First the principal gave a really
long talk, and then the school
orchestra played some music. I
think it was called *"A Little Sleep
Music,"* or something like that.

Then we were divided up into our classes. I'm in
class 5B, the same class as Cheyenne, which is
awesome!!! ☺

Cheyenne is my **very best friend,** since kindergarten! And this is because:

Cheyenne →

1. We like the same **games**
   (Burial, for instance. To play it,
   we always take Cheyenne's sister,
   Chanelle, and bury her in the sandbox).

2. We find the same things **funny**
   (like, that time a TV was thrown
   out of an upstairs window of
   Cheyenne's building).

3. Cheyenne is totally brave and always
   says the **craziest things**
   (I'm still working on this).

4. We like to eat the same things
   (our favorites are **crackers with
   peanut butter, and potato chips
   from a can.** Really though, Cheyenne
   likes to eat everything).

5. Cheyenne is really good at **keeping a secret**
   (She knew who put the earthworm in Mrs.
   Bohner's salami sandwich. I mean, come on!
   Why did I get a D for my really great picture
   in art class?).

6. We looove **animals!!!**

animals

That's why we absolutely had to be in the same class. Otherwise, I just would have gone home right away.

stern look --→

Our new teacher took us to our classroom. She's kind of small and has very short hair. And really narrow glasses that she's always peering over with a stern expression.

The first thing she did was look fiercely over her glasses.

That immediately made all of us stop talking.

"**My name is Ginny Crabbert,**" she said with that same expression, so that no one even dared wiggle his ears.

"**You don't know it yet, so I'm telling you now. I will not tolerate anyone cracking jokes about my name.**"

We all just stared at her. 🙂
Except for Cheyenne. "Hee-hee-hee," she giggled.

Ginny Crabbert is a crab.

giggle...

→ She had to stay after school
for that one. 🙁

Even on our very **first** day at the **Wilt Whatman Middle School.**

On top of which, Cheyenne's arm is in a cast, so she couldn't write anything as punishment anyway.

Cheyenne and I nudged each other and Cheyenne pretended she was going to throw up.

But in secret, so that Mrs. Crabbert wouldn't see it.

And that was why we almost missed hearing her say that we all should find our own seats.

Suddenly everybody started dashing around. Cheyenne and me, too, of course, because, we absolutely, positively wanted to sit next to each other by the window.

As far in the back of the room as possible.

our seats

Two boys almost got our seats, but Cheyenne **hissed** at them and they left.

At the back wall, five or six boys were trying to squeeze together at one table.

That made Mrs. Crabbert **really mad,** and she divided them up all over the classroom.

No one dared to complain. At some point everything got quiet again, and we all stared straight ahead.

In the very front of the room sat one single girl.

stuck-up
nose --→

She had long blonde hair and really cool clothes. And a totally stuck-up nose.

Cheyenne didn't say a word for the rest of the hour. She just covered her new workbook with lots and lots of drawings of rabbits. But they looked more like amoebas, because Cheyenne can't draw with her left hand.

Mrs. Crabbert tried the whole time to get us to play some games meant to break the ice, but no one was brave enough to speak.

Then finally the bell rang for recess. Yes! The class headed to the playground. All of the girls gathered in one spot. I only knew Cheyenne and two other girls from my old school.

So, I was in California for summer vacation.

And I learned how to kitesurf.

Almost all of the girls surrounded her. I was tempted to join them, even though I have no idea what kitesurfing is.

Then Cheyenne interrupted her to say that she had spent her summer going to the swimming pool.

Then I totally crashed coming down the ← water slide and broke my arm. Blam!

Blam!

And waved her cast around.

I didn't say anything about my summer vacation. We had rented a cottage in Maine. But with a family like mine, 🙁 it really doesn't matter where we go! SERIOUSLY!

Before   After

Take today, for example, at lunchtime. We all went out to eat together, because it's a special day when you start a new school.
So I got to choose where we went to eat.
And I wanted pizza!

Dad immediately started grumbling that he had wanted to take us out to the Greek restaurant. Because he wants to eat calamari again.

But this was **my** first day at the **Wilt Whatman Middle School**, and so we went to the Italian restaurant. 😄

My brothers cheered and whacked me on the back with their space weapons. They meant to be nice. But I hit them back anyway.

Simon

Jacob

My brothers' names are Simon and Jacob. They're both eight. And they're **tWins.** Eight-year-old twin brothers are the **Worst** siblings you can have. Trust me on this.

When we're in the car, I always have to sit in the middle. So that the two of them won't fight so much. But they fight anyway. And, of course, I'm the one who gets hit.

The whole way to the Italian restaurant I had
a lightsaber up my nose.
Or a space gun in my ear. Especially when Dad
went over a bump.

I think he tried extra hard
to go over the biggest bump.

But I didn't care, because I was totally looking forward to having pizza! Mom's always cooking Indian dishes lately, with chickpeas and carrot curry and stuff.

hee-hee-hee

I ordered a pepperoni pizza, and so did the boys. Dad ordered calamari, of course. He's really stubborn about that. When he wants calamari, he wants calamari.

And that funky wine he drinks, that smells like a wild pig has peed on a pine tree.

After we ordered, Jacob knocked the candle that was stuck in a bottle off the table with his lightsaber.
By accident, of course.

thump

But Dad got **stinking mad** anyway. And when he's **stinking mad**, we're in for it.

Then it was Mom's turn. "Why are you always bouncing up and down on your chair? It drives me crazy," Dad said, grumbling at her.

"I'm not bouncing. That's my new shiatsu pillow. It has two rotating cushions that relax your muscles and keep you from getting headaches."

shiatsu pillow

Mom's voice TREMBLED a little when she said this.
Because she was bouncing UP and down a bit.

Dad sighed. "Don't tell me you've ordered another piece of junk from TV again! I've already had it with that jeweled fountain with the water pump and light that you brought home recently."

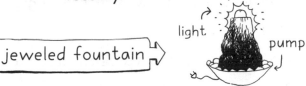

light

jeweled fountain

pump

Mom didn't answer, and I had to grin. Dad actually has no idea what all Mom really buys. Let me just mention the:

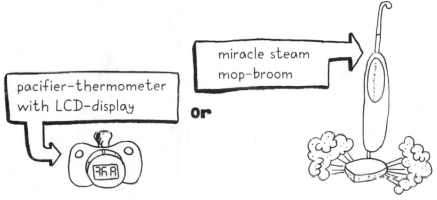

miracle steam mop-broom

pacifier-thermometer with LCD-display

or

Finally our food arrived and I thought, now things will be great. "The calamari looks like **whale buttholes**," I said, just to cheer things up a bit.

But Dad, I guess, was in a bad mood. He didn't find that funny at all.

Next Simon knocked over his apple juice, right onto my pizza. Of course. And Mom tried like crazy to scrub the pizza with every single napkin on the table.

Unfortunately, the pizza tasted a little mushy after that.

And it tasted like the little green-white-red napkin bits that were stuck to it, too.

22

Then, just when I thought things had calmed down again, a slice of Jacob's pizza fell into Dad's wild pig pee, I mean, wine, by accident. The whole glass tipped over, right onto his calamari.

Dad was really steamed by now, and there weren't any more napkins left.

But Mom couldn't have scrubbed anything anyway, because she had pushed the wrong button on her shiatsu pillow.

I think she was a little *jittery*.
And her pillow was, too. Anyway, Mom suddenly started bouncing up and down on her chair like crazy.
Everybody in the restaurant was staring, and one little boy even pointed his finger at us.

It was the perfect time to ask if I could have an ice cream.

When we got home, Mom had a present for me. Because, after all, it was a special day. And suddenly I was super **excited.**

Mom acted really mysterious, and said it was something very unique. That she had found in a little Indian shop.

"When I was buying Ayurvedic ----->
massage oil.

And Pan Parag Gum
Cleanser and Breath
Freshener -------->

What?

And Haldiram Chana Dal
spicy roasted
chickpea halves."

Still, I was **excited.** But it was a strange kind of excited. I unpacked it and felt a little sick. 😐

It was a **recorDer.** ----→

I need to explain something
here. I am the **worst
recorDer player** in the
world.

I am **totally aWful,**
recorder-wise.

To me, all notes sound
equal—**equally aWful.**

I've been taking lessons for three years now, and in that time I've worn out **SEVEN RECORDER TEACHERS:**

1. **MRS. ACKERMANN.** Suffered sudden hearing loss and had to retire.

2. **MS. HUPPERT.** Moved. Address unknown.

3. **MR. TRAVINI.** One day there was a Rottweiler in his garden, along with a sign on his fence that said: **Beware biting dog. Do not enter yard.**

4. **MRS. PHELPS.** Changed jobs to work behind the meat counter at the grocery store.

5. **MRS. BRANT.** Sent me down to the basement to get a recorder cleaner, then locked the door. Luckily, I could escape through a window well.

6. **MRS. JONES.** Moved to New Zealand.

7. **MRS. COHEN.** I could never understand her, because she muttered a lot after I played. No idea why she suddenly disappeared.

I hate playinG the recorDer!

That's why I would have been much happier with a dog, for example, or a little sheep.

Because, honestly, I would really, really like to have a pet of my own.

The next time we celebrate my first day at school, I definitely will have to make that clear ahead of time. It's also bad for Mom when I don't like her presents so much.
And for Nana Ingrid as well.

Nana Ingrid

diary

Nana is the one who gave me this diary.
She told me that I could trust it with all my little secrets.

Does she think, maybe, that I don't have a best friend?

That evening, I wanted to watch my favorite TV show. - - - - - - - - - - →

Okay, but first you have to practice the recorder.

It was seven o'clock and the *CREDITS* were already on!

But Mom had her **Don't-argue-with-me** look on. And I knew what that meant.

So I sat down in front of the TV and blew into my new recorder. It sounded exactly like my old recorder. Horrible!

Shelley and Ashley were moving their mouths on the tv, but I couldn't understand what they were saying.

And that's why I tried to play especially fast. I knew I could be finished in three minutes.

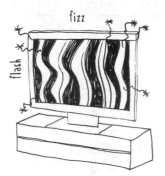

Then something really strange happened. All of a sudden the TV screen started to flash and fizz and just disappeared.

Instead, some old guy with an ugly tie was sitting there. Next to his left ear were the words **Market Report.**

CHANGE THE CHANNEL, change it right now!

No one was around. I went to change the channel myself, but it already was on the **right** channel.

The cool girls had simply disappeared!

The TV must have been BROKEN. I jumped up to get Dad, so he could fix it, and that was when I tripped over Webster, the turtle. →

trip
Webster

(I'll write something about Webster later. Right now I'm too **stinking mad!**)

ow!

whump!

Unfortunately, Dad was right in the middle of preparing something for his class, and didn't want to come over to the TV. He just mumbled something about a *stupid show.*

SATURDAY, AUGUST 20

I woke up 😑 😑 in the middle of the night
because something hard was poking me in the
back. I turned on the light ☀️ and looked
under the covers.

It was the **new recorDer!** ----→
Mom probably had snuck
it into the bed with me.

That was **STRANGE**, I thought.
What did she think I would do? Play in
my sleep?

Maybe some night I should slip a
food crisper ➤ or a chocolate fountain
under her pillow, so she would see
how weird that is!

zzz...

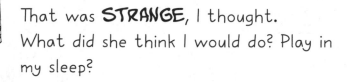

MONDAY, AUGUST 22

In our first hour today, Mrs. Crabbert wanted us to write a personal profile. Mine looked like this:

Name: Lotta Petermann
Age: 10
Eye color: Blue with a little green and brown around the edges
Favorite Animal: Dogs, really small sheep
Favorite Book: ~~Encyk Animal Encykloat~~ Matilda
Favorite Food: Crackers with peanut butter and stacked chips, pancakes
What I Like: ANIMALS!!, my best friend Cheyenne, vacation
What I Don't Like: RECORDERS! and Brussels sprouts

Mrs. Crabbert read this and then said to me (this is really true!):

> Oh, you play the recorder, Lotta? That's wonderful. Please bring it with you tomorrow, and you can play something for the class.

WHAT? She must need new glasses! **I don't like,** that's what I wrote!

UGH, I'm already sick of that weird Ginny Crabbert and the **Wilt Whatman Middle School.**

WeirD

WeirDer

The only good thing is recess, when all the girls stand around together and talk about all kinds of things. The one with the long blonde hair is Bernadette Bester. She's pretty rich, I think. Because at recess she told everyone she has a horse. And then she flipped her long blonde hair.

flip

A crossbred mare. Her name is Secret.

You mean like the *DEODORANT?*

I don't think that Bernadette will be speaking to her anymore. 😛

But Cheyenne didn't even notice that she had **offended** Bernadette. And then she announced that she had **two hundred** rabbits at home.

Well, nobody believed that. 😐
I quickly whispered to her that the others might not want to play with her anymore if she keeps on saying such funny things.

But that didn't matter much to her, I think. She just walked off and found the absolute **coolest** boy on the playground. He just had to sign her cast, she said. His name was **Kevin**.

Cheyenne said he even drew a little heart on it for her, but really it looks like his pen slipped when he was dotting his i.
I think Kevin just scribbled it.

brother

Later when Bernadette saw it, she got a funny expression on her face. Because, Kevin is her **BROTHER.**

And by the way: that part about the 200 rabbits—it's really true!
That afternoon I was at Cheyenne's. She lives in sort of a small apartment in a tall building.

Cheyenne lives here

They don't need much room,
because there's no father
there to spread his stuff out
everywhere, like mine does.

And her mother doesn't take up much space,
either. She's tired most of the time and lies on
the sofa.

Cheyenne shares a room
with her sister, Chanelle.
Chanelle is seven and
really **ANNOYING.**

Now that I think about it, there are at least ten things I find much **more annoyinG.** 😣
Namely:

1. two little **Brothers!!!** ☠

2. the **SounD** that comes out of my **RecorDer** 🎵

3. Ginny **Crabbert**

4. Dad's **sChool-teaCher voice** when he wants to explain something to somebody

5. all the **stuff** that Mom's always buying so that there's no money left over for a dog (or even a very small sheep)

6. **HoMeWork:** particularly Math and Language Arts

7. **BernaDette,** and all of the kitesurting and her deodor-horse

8. Mom's Indian **Ayu-Whatever** -Dishes

9. **Webster,** the turtle, who's always lying around in the way.

10. Err...

39

Cheyenne and Chanelle's entire room was full of rabbits! They were hopping all over the place, and sitting at the bottom of their closet, on top of Chanelle's pillow, and behind the TV.

I spotted a few of them lying under the bed and inside a gym bag, but they looked a little stiff. Like **MUMMIES**. I wished I hadn't looked at them so closely.

Then Chanelle started screaming
This is nothing new. She screams
most of the time.

We do have two
boy rabbits!
Charlie and **Teenie**,
can't you see that
they're boys?

And Cheyenne and I just looked at each
other and grinned. Chanelle acts pretty
young and silly sometimes.

Cheyenne named her rabbit Teenie, because she loves the cartoon show, *TEENIE THE WEENIE*

He's always going on hot dog adventures because he's going to be grilled and he'd rather avoid it.

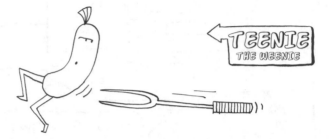

Cheyenne knows a lot about stuff like that. About TV and stars and so on. Much more than I do. I guess it's because **I just turned ten,** and Cheyenne has been **ten for forever.**

Still, I know more about animals. I know, for instance, that it is totally UNFAIR that Cheyenne has so many animals and I don't have a single one.

And her rabbits are so sweet!

I tried to pick one up, but it hid behind a big pile of clothes that were lying in one corner of the room.

"What's something you can't see that smells like carrots?" Cheyenne asked. I didn't know, but then Chanelle yelled: "A rabbit fart!"

We laughed so hard that all of the rabbits ran off and hid.

Cheyenne knows a whole lot of funny jokes.

But there was something strange about having all those rabbits in one room. So I asked Cheyenne if her mother got **angry** about all the rabbits all over the place.

And the *rabbit* poop everywhere.

Cheyenne just shook her head and looked quite proud. "Nope. Mommy's always driving us to Burger Paradise and we buy hamburgers and the rabbits get the lettuce."

Cool! That's something I can only dream of. Dad always gets in a **bad mood** if I even think about uttering the word "dog."

Then something occurred to me. What if Cheyenne and Chanelle gave me one of their rabbits, since they have so many. 😄
⇨ **Just one.** 🐰

But when I asked Cheyenne, she gave me a funny look. She's so business-minded.

And then she asked what she would get for it.

Suddenly I got a lump in my throat. "I'm your best friend," I said. "And you have so many rabbits! Surely you could give me just one!"

Cheyenne has so much stuff anyway, her own **camera cell phone,** an **MP3 player,** and a **TV** in her room! With a **Nintendo Wii!**

——⟶ All I have is Mom's **old cassette player.** 😐

Why'D she Get so stinGy?
she really DiDn't Want to Give me even one!

So I jumped up and yelled that she should just
find herself a new best friend. And I announced
that I was going to sit on the first row next to
Bernadette the next day. If there was still room,
that is.

**So
there!**

Cheyenne and Chanelle started whispering to
each other, and then Cheyenne pulled a rabbit
out from among a bunch of dolls.

Okay, here.
This is
Scrappy.
You can
have him.

wobble

Kevin

Scrappy had **funny** back legs. →
They just hung down.

"What's wrong with him?"
I asked **grumpily**. I didn't
want Cheyenne to think that I was her
best friend again.

She told me that a few days ago Chanelle had
gotten her foot tangled up in the TV cord.

cord

TV from
the back

b
a
h
g
!!

Scrappy

"And the whole thing came crashing down, and
unfortunately **Scrappy's** legs were under it."

So then I just turned around and slammed the door behind me 〔BAMM!〕 and ran out. It really made me sad that Cheyenne was so mean! But I'll show her. **TomorroW I'm GoinG to look for a new best frienD!**

When I got home I acted like nothing was wrong.
Leave it to Mom to notice something anyway.
She wanted to make me feel better. So she gave
me a bag of **chips.**

"I bought them from a home-shopping
station on TV a little while ago," she
said, as if that would cheer me up.
"Chicken Chips: Ideal for Healthy Teeth.
I think they sound really delicious. And so healthy!"

"Oh, Mom," I sniffled,
"they're for dogs!"
Mom said, **"Oh,"** and suddenly
looked quite worried.

Because we don't have a dog.

"And I bought a 20-pack.
How annoying," she
murmured.
Then she turned pale.

And the
boys and
I already
had some...

So I went to my room and the first thing I saw was my **recorder.** ---->
It was lying on the rug, smack dab in the middle of the room.

That could mean only one thing: Jacob and Simon had been in my room and TOUCHED my things!

That is SO not okay!
Why else would I have a **SiGn** on my door, in extra-large letters?

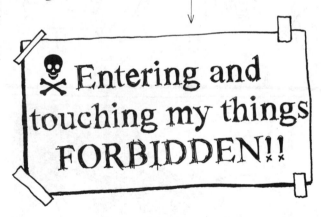

☠ Entering and touching my things FORBIDDEN!!

I grabbed the recorder and swung it like a club.
"Where are you?" I roared, and ran into their room.

On the way, I stumbled over Webster, the turtle.

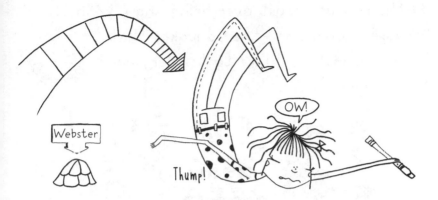

(I'll write something about Webster later. Right now I'm much too **stinking mad!!!**)

Jacob and Simon weren't in their room. **ARGH!** Lucky for them.

I couldn't get anything out of Mom. She'd been reading the **Chicken Chips: Ideal for Healthy Teeth** bag the whole time. And looked pretty **WORRIED**.

The twins didn't surface until later that evening. By then I was almost over being angry with them because I could smell the pancakes that Mom was making. I had to try very hard to be really mad.

But then my two pesky brothers dared to claim that they hadn't been in my room at all that afternoon, and said I should just throw my recorder in the toilet anyway, where it belonged.

Ha! This calleD for immeDiate revenGe.

So I ran after them with my recorder and tooted at them so loud that they ran to Mom.

"Stop that!" Mom cried, and made
her **stinking mad** face. ------>

"Why?" I said, "I'm just practicing
my recorder."

 And then I kept tooting until the
pancakes were served.

Mmm, pancakes. Delicious! ☺
I was almost in a good mood again.

#No.1#

Pancakes are my absolute favorite food
(besides crackers with peanut butter and chips,
of course).

Favorite food
#No.1b#

But then I spit the first bite out on my plate
again! What had Mom done this time?

The pancakes were ruined!
They tasted like...
Brussels sprouts! Yuck!

Lotta! That's the last straw! If you're going to eat like a pig, then go to your ROOM!

I was totally **annoyeD!**

But I can't eat these! Mom used mealy flour. And eggs with bird flu! They taste totally *horrible!*

Now both Mom and Dad were in **bad moods!**

Strangely, their pancakes tasted delicious. At any rate, they ate all of them. Mine were the only ones that tasted like **Brussels sprouts!**

Jacob and Simon gobbled down their pancakes
too. And they don't like Brussels sprouts, either.

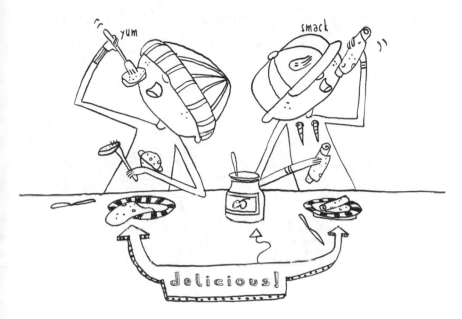

So I only licked off the applesauce.
Though it was a little **yucky** too.

Kind of like **cat food.**

Luckily, in my room I had
hidden an entire **mega-sized
bar of chocolate.**

Which was almost as good as **pancakes!**

TUESDAY, AUGUST 23

Today in school I acted as if Cheyenne simply DIDN'T EXIST. Unfortunately I don't think she even noticed, because she kept talking to me the whole time anyway.

So I sat down next to a boy named Paul. ------------> Paul wears brainy glasses and looks nice. I suspect he's somebody good to copy from.

brainy glasses

TEST

Emma   Bernadette   Maggie

There weren't <u>any</u> seats left next to Bernadette. They'd already been taken by Emma and Maggie.

58

In Language Arts, Mrs. Crabbert said I should play something on my recorder.
Yeah, well, I mistakenly left my recorder at home. **Too bad!**

 Then Mrs. Crabbert looked into my backpack, because it was open, and asked:

And what is this?

It was the recorder. **OH NO!**

I know for a fact that I hadn't put it there! It must have been **Mom**! I was so shocked that I couldn't think of an excuse.

"Which song would you like to play for us?" Mrs. Crabbert asked, once I got to the blackboard at the front of the class. My legs were **SHAKING!**

WHICH SONG? WHERE DID SHE GET THE IDEA THAT I COULD PLAY SONGS??

Hei-ho-Teenie

Cheyenne whispered to me. That's her favorite song. But I acted as if she just **DIDN'T EXIST.**

Then I blew into the recorder.

Everybody immediately put their hands over their ears.

I wanted to do that too, but I needed both hands to play the recorder. And then I saw everyone suddenly get a funny look on their faces. SHOCKED. But some of them also were grinning. And they were all looking at the board. So I stopped playing and turned around.

And there, written in chalk, were the words:

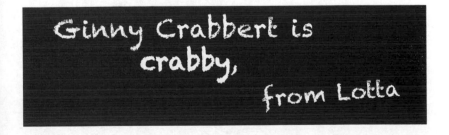

Ginny Crabbert is crabby,

from Lotta

I got a funny feeling
in my stomach.
"That wasn't me!"
I squeaked.

Mrs. Crabbert looked
around the classroom
with an **anGry
expression,**

but she didn't scold anyone,
because no one would admit
to writing it. Instead she
GlareD at me and told me
to go back to my seat.

We practiced our handwriting for the rest of
the day.

Anyway, I really want an **ANIMAL!** I'm definitely planning on it. And for that I don't need Cheyenne. I don't want some boring rabbit, instead...

yawn!

I'd like to have a really small sheep.

Mom and Dad will never allow that.

On top of which, our garden is way too small. I also know that really small sheep gets **really big** at some point. After all, I'm not a **fool**.

And besides, what would I do with all that wool?

A cat 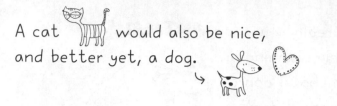 would also be nice,
and better yet, a dog.

A Jack Rustle Terrier (or whatever they're called).
My Aunt Sarah has one.

And I want one, too.

Aunt Sarah

her real
Jack-Rustle-
Terrier

my
**Dream-
Terrier**

After school, Cheyenne came over to me and said
that if I wanted, I could pick out a rabbit. Or
two. A boy and a girl.

And soon I would have
two hundred, too.

Then I was totally happy.

 Because, honestly, I didn't
want to be mad at Cheyenne
anymore.

Maybe rabbits aren't so boring after all.

Actually, I wanted to go right over to Cheyenne's.
But then I thought it might be better
to first tell Mom the **great news**
that we were getting two rabbits.

I also knew exactly how I wanted to tell her: First, I would ask for a really small sheep, because I thought Mom would be happy that, instead of giving me a sheep, she wouldn't have to give me anything, because Cheyenne was giving me the rabbits.

But Mom was not happy. She didn't want me to have any pets **at all!**

She said that first I had to be old enough to take responsibility for a pet myself, and that she wasn't at all interested in having to buy food for it and take care of it, and on and on and on.

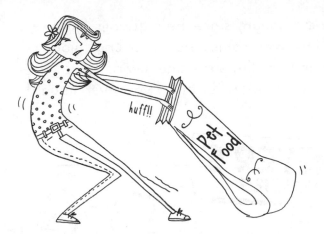

Of course I said right away that she definitely wouldn't have to do that, because I would take care of the sheep.

 Or the rabbits.

Then Mom said that we already had a pet. Namely, Webster, the turtle.  And that I didn't take care of him, either.

But Webster isn't a real pet! He's at least a **thousand years old**, and I'm pretty sure he died a long time ago. I had proof. He never moves. I don't even remember what his head looks like anymore, because it's always inside his shell.

It's **strange** though, since he's always lying around in the way somewhere, so that you stumble over him. I'm sure the twins have something to do with it, but I've never caught them at it.

I asked Mom if I could have a dog, if I could prove that Webster was dead.

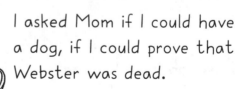

So then she sent me to my room and told me to do my homework.

I'm getting a little **impatient!** Mom doesn't want a dog only because then she'd have to buy dog food, and couldn't spend all our money on all sorts of **WeirD stuff!**

Like, for instance, the *apple-corer,* she just bought:

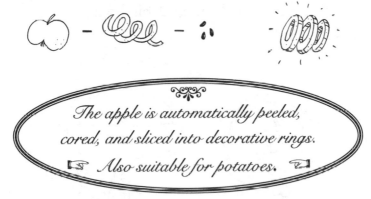

> *The apple is automatically peeled, cored, and sliced into decorative rings.*
>
> ☞ *Also suitable for potatoes.* ☜

I don't want decorative potato rings. Ever. I want a pet!

Webster

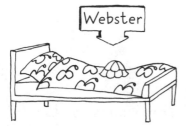

When I got to my room, Webster was lying on my bed. There's no way in the world he could have climbed up there himself. **REVEN9E!**

grrrr!!!

Luckily I was already **furious.** I ran into Jacob and Simon's room.

They were sitting there on the floor, filling my recorder with **MUSTARD.**

Jacob tried to hide it behind his back, but it was already too late.

bling

mustard

I grabbed Fishy and Barney and ran to the window and held them outside it.

Jacob and Simon turned on the waterworks, of course, and immediately started screaming for Mom.

Fishy and Barney are their favorite stuffed animals, and they can't go to sleep without them.

Fishy is a whale (at least, that's what Jacob claims, though Fishy looks more like a flounder), and Barney is a monkey.

Barney

Dangle

MERCY!

HELP

Fishy

I dangled them this way and that and they begged for mercy.

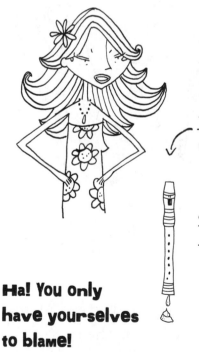

Then Mom arrived, and the fun was over. She looked ready to yell at me, but I showed her the recorder with the mustard.

So she decided to yell at the boys instead.

Ha! You only have yourselves to blame!

On the way back to my room, I stumbled over Webster.

First I wanted to pick him up and stuff him in Mom's crisper.

```
Battery operated.
Press button to turn on.
Keeps food fresher longer.
Capacity: 5 quarts
```

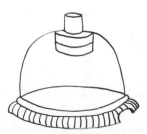

But then it occurred to me that I didn't want to keep Webster fresh at all.

So instead, I made a plan.

⇩ I wanted to earn my own money.

⇩ And then I wanted to buy my own pet, with my own money!

⇩ I would care for it all by myself, and take full responsibility for it.

⇩ **So there!**

Once that was clear, I thought about how I would earn money. Maybe my recorder was worth something? Except not stuffed with mustard.

So I took it into the bathroom and rinsed it out.

Mom sometimes sells things on eBay, but I suspect she won't help me sell my recorder.

We'll see. 😐

There's gotta be someone who **desperately** needs a recorder.

sigh!

For the time being, I put it back on the shelf over my bed.

That night when I went to bed, I tried to dream
about my dog.

Instead all I could dream about was my room
being full of rabbits.
You couldn't even see the rug, there were so
many. Yet they were baa-ing so sweetly, just like
little sheep.

WEDNESDAY, AUGUST 24

In the middle of the night, my recorder jumped down on me! **I swear!**

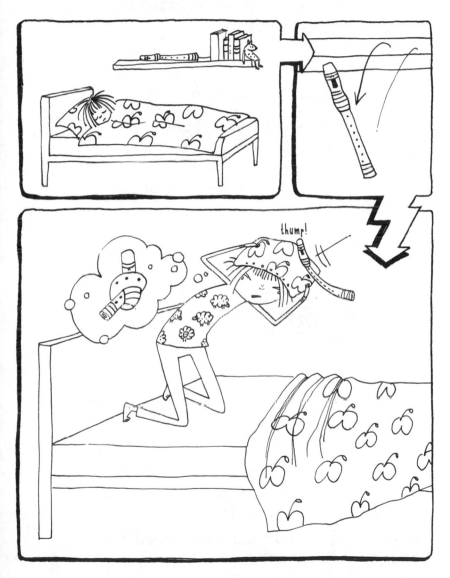

THURSDAY, AUGUST 25

So, today I start earning money!
We have a neighbor, *Mrs. Lopez*.
She's an old lady, and has a little dog.
The dog's name is **Polly**.

I planned to ring Mrs. Lopez's doorbell and tell her that I was going to start walking Polly every day from now on. I was sure that Mrs. Lopez would be happy that she doesn't have to do that anymore, and can look after her rheumatism and her artificial hip instead, or whatever it is that old ladies need to look after.

And then she'll give me **a lot of money.** It's a
perfect plan, I'm sure!

So that afternoon, I rang
Mrs. Lopez's bell.

Mrs. Lopez looked at me with such
weird lines in her forehead, when
I explained to her that now she
could sit in her armchair and knit
support hose, because I was going
to walk Polly.

She put her hands on her hips, and scowled at
me. And then acted like she wasn't an old lady
at all.

I like to walk Polly all by myself, thank you very much.

she said, and tried to close the door.

I quickly stuck my foot in it and said:

Oh, please! Just for today!

I ♡ Pets

And Mrs. Lopez looked like she was considering it. In the background I could hear bloodcurdling **SCREECHING** sounds, like someone was being murdered. But I knew it was only Hannibal, Ms. Lopez's parrot.

Actually, he's not a parrot at all, but a cockatiel, a **Nymphicus hollandicus,** as Mom once told me. I think that means that he's got something wrong with his nymph glands.

SCREECH!

SCREECH!!

The nymphs are located somewhere around here and here.

Then Mrs. Lopez said that, actually, she could use me today. Because she wants to play tennis.

The senior championships were coming up on the weekend, and she needed to train for it so that she could beat her old opponent, **Helen Jansen.** Then she pretended like she was going to hit a ball with her tennis racket.

grrrrr

Oh, man, I don't know if tennis is all that healthy for old ladies. But the main thing is that I get to walk Polly.

yippee

We only needed to settle the finances. I told her that I would accept **ten dollars** → an hour.

Mrs. Lopez got that funny expression on her face again and said that she would pay me  ← **three dollars** and not a cent more.

Now I was getting **REALLY mAd!** That's not the kind of thing an old granny would do, right?

Old grannies are supposed to be happy when they can give young people money.

After all, they already have everything, dogs and parrots and so on.

HOW CAN SOmEONE BE SO STINgY?

I tried to bargain with her, but she wouldn't budge. 😞

BUT NO, mRS. LOPEz WAS TOTALLY dISAPPOINTINg AS AN OLd gRANNY!

Still, Polly is really **sweet!** She's one of those dogs where you can't tell which end is her front and which is her back.

Luckily Mrs. Lopez knew. She put Polly's leash on at the right end, and told me that under **no circumstances** was I to let Polly off the leash, because she immediately would **RUN OFF.** 😐

And then I set out. 😄
The first thing I did was to go over to
Cheyenne's and ring her doorbell. Unfortunately,
she wasn't there. 🙁

Then I went to the park and the playground.
Polly trotted along behind me.

I think she's older than Mrs. Lopez, a real doggy
granny. Actually, I almost had to pull her along,
she was moving so slow. Like a **log on four legs.**

snore ...

When we got to the park, I decided to let her off the leash after all. And then **A WHOLE LOT OF THINGS** happened at once.

1. Polly **IMMEDIATELY** ran off, and went right to the PLAYGROUND.

2. She knocked down at least **FOUR LITTLE KIDS**. x 4

3. She crouched down in the SANDBOX and left a **REALLY BIG POOP** (impressive since she's a pretty small dog). ewww!

4. She found a few **DOGGIE TREATS** in somebody's handbag.

5. She **BIT** a woman who wanted to take the treats away from her. bite mark

6. She ran to the pond and **JUMPED IN**.

7. She chased **DUCKS**.

8. She swam back with a **DUCK IN HER MOUNTH**. That's called relieving. I know that because I know so much about dogs. (Oh wait, that's called retrieving.)

In the meantime, ten or twenty mothers started screaming. As if something BAD had happened.

scream!

whoosh!

I just wanted to go home and pretend like I didn't have anything to do with any of this. But then I would have gotten into trouble with Mrs. Lopez. So I had to go over to them. ☹

The mothers were really mad at me, and said things like, "HORRIBLE," "IRRESPONSIBLE," and "POLICE."

I fished an old plastic bag out of a garbage can and put the dog poop in it. ⟶ It was sooooo DISGUSTING.

By the time I had done that, Polly was in the pond again. And again, there was a lot of screaming.

I couldn't exactly jump in the pond, so I tried to get Polly to come to me with some **Chicken Chips: Ideal for Healthy Teeth,** that I found in my backpack. But apparently Polly is not interested in dental care.

Then I threw a stick into the pond.
Okay, the stick was actually my
recorder. I had brought it with me.
I threw it as far out as I could.

Mostly because I didn't want that recorder
pouncing on me at night again. ☺

☺ But I hadn't counted on Polly.

Polly left the ducks in peace and lunged
at the recorder.

Then she swam over to the bank, dropped it at my feet, and shook herself so hard that I got totally soaked. ⊖

sprinkle!

spray!

shake!

I quickly slipped her leash back on her. Unfortunately she had a lot of duckweed in her coat and she smelled a little **gross**.

Suddenly I was afraid that Mrs. Lopez wouldn't pay me if I brought Polly back smelling like a swamp. 😐

So I ran home to wash her. Mom was busy at the moment. She was hanging onto her MAGIC FITNESS POWER TRAINER, training her stomach, her legs, and her rear end.

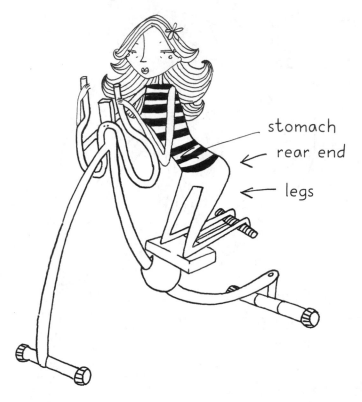

stomach

← rear end

← legs

The whole thing looked so **complicated** that I didn't want to bother her.

I went looking for the shampoo.
The shampoo bottle next to
the tub was almost <u>empty</u>, and
Polly has a lot of hair.

I didn't find any more
shampoo, but I did find a
huge bucket of *SUPER
ROCKET POWDER—*
**Self-Cleaning Foam for
the Toilet.**

Self-cleaning, cool!

That meant that I didn't have to scrub Polly
myself, the *ROCKET POWDER* would do that
for me!

bubbles

bling!

I put her in the bathtub, wet her down, and sprinkled a cup of **Power Foam for the Toilet** on her.

BOOYAH, IT REALLY FOAMED!

I couldn't see Polly at all anymore, and the ball of foam in the bathtub kept growing bigger and bigger, and bubbled and fizzed. But then Polly gave such a pitiful whimper that I wanted to rinse her off.

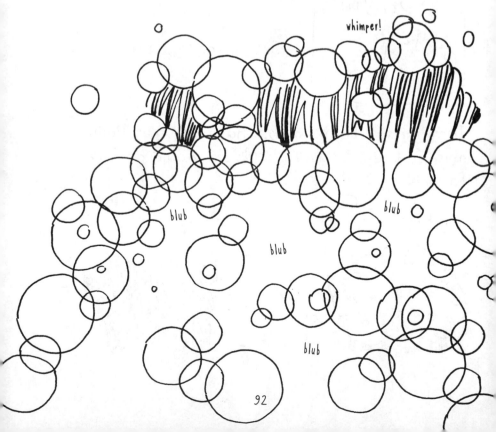

And then my heart did a somersault. **HONEST!**
Suddenly, Polly looked really *bizarre*.

Her coat had gotten so thin and
fuzzy, and was sticking out in all
directions, like one of those really
hairy cactuses. ------------→

And for some reason it also was a little blue,
just a little bit, but even so.
She didn't look at all like Polly anymore!

Oh no! Mrs. Lopez was never going to believe
that this was really her dog! ☺

And of course
there was no
way I was going
to make **any** money.

blub   93

I tried to smooth down Polly's hair, and rubbed her coat with some of **Mom's skin cream,** ---→ but that just made things worse.

MORE SPIKY, somehow. And then I couldn't wash the skin cream out.

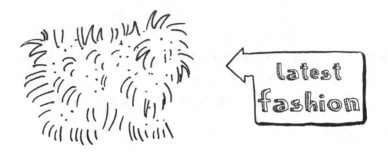

latest fashion

When I looked at her, I got a really thick lump in my throat. But then I had a good idea. I'd tell Mrs. Lopez that I had been to the dog salon with Polly, and that a fuzzy blue coat was the **latest fashion** for dogs.

Then Ms. Lopez would surely pay me the ten dollars.

Maybe even more!

I was pretty satisfied with myself, and gave
Polly a few more spikes with the face cream. ☺

Now she looked like a cross between
cotton candy and a **porcupine.**

But still,
pretty good!

When we arrived back at Mrs. Lopez's, I was feeling really proud of myself. Unfortunately, Mrs. Lopez was in a fairly crabby mood.

She probably had lost her tennis game against her old opponent, **Helen Jansen**. But that was no reason to start yelling at me and **chase me off.** And she didn't give me any money, either.

Helen Jansen

Despite the fact that I had given Polly a new hairdo, one that no other dog in the whole world has, and for free. **Mrs. Lopez is truly the stingiest person I know!!**

FRIDAY, AUGUST 26TH

After school today, Cheyenne came over to my house.

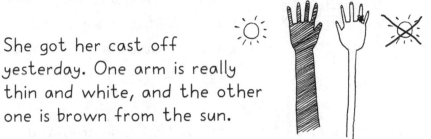

She got her cast off yesterday. One arm is really thin and white, and the other one is brown from the sun.

And she even brought a **rabbit** for me with her.
It looked so sweet!

I ran to Mom right away, and asked her if I could keep it.

I thought that if she saw it, she couldn't say no. I put it in the fruit dish right under her nose, where it very *sweetly* nibbled on an apple.

But Mom said NO anyway, and was really annoyed about it. She thought she had made it clear that the subject was closed, she said. And that I should be reasonable about it. ⊖

So I ran out of the room with Cheyenne, and thought about hiding my rabbit somewhere in our garden. But our garden is pretty small and there are **no** places to hide.

Here?

or here?

or maybe here

And Cheyenne even said I could have her rabbit cage. She and Chanelle had to give their rabbits away, because her mother had noticed how many of them there were.

They want to sell them all, and I could come with them to help. And I'd even earn some **money** for it.

I thought that was totally cool.

And of course I wanted to help.

So I ran to my room and grabbed my **recorder.**

Then, with Cheyenne and my rabbit, and with the recorder in my backpack, I ran over to the building where Cheyenne lives.

Cheyenne lives here

Chanelle was already there, with a huge cardboard box with a picture of a TV on it.

And the box was full of rabbits!

They were scurrying around and squeaking and scratching and looking really cute.

Chanelle was sitting in the grass on a wool blanket, and was eating a piece of bread with jelly. She was sticking stickers from a box into her sticker album, which was covered in **STAINS.**

The rabbits are inside here

Rabbits $10

rattle!

"Let's see how many you've sold already," Cheyenne said, and grabbed the **piggy bank** and shook it.

"Nothing yet," Chanelle mumbled, dribbling a little jelly onto her pink glitter t-shirt.

Then Cheyenne moved the price sign so that people could see it better.

So, now we'll get rich.

Rabbits $10

I leaned my recorder up against the box. And added these words to the sign:

Rabbits $10

magic recorder $50

Then I wanted to know how much of the money I would get. Cheyenne said I could keep the money I made on my rabbit and on **Scrappy**.

And again, I found that a little **GreeDy!**

But luckily I had an *idea*. Namely, in my backpack I had a few bags of **Chicken Chips: Ideal for Healthy Teeth** left over from Polly.

    Three full bags, plus one that had been opened.

Because I know that Cheyenne and Chanelle are almost always hungry, I sold them the chips. **One bag for one rabbit.**

At first they didn't want to trade a whole rabbit for the bag that was open, but I <u>didn't</u> give in.

Ha! Now I had **five-and-a-half rabbits** to sell (I won't get more than five dollars at the most for Scrappy).

That's **fifty-five dollars total!**

Plus the **recorder.** Could I get a dog for that? With dog food and a collar and leash?

Maybe a really little one, at least?

Cheyenne and Chanelle thought the **Chicken Chips: Ideal for Healthy Teeth,** were totally delicious.

crunch

When they'd finished the **Chicken Chips** we still hadn't sold even one rabbit.

"We need to move closer to the street," I said, and so we pulled the cardboard box with the rabbits over to the sidewalk.

Rabbits, rabbits, beautiful rabbits!

A lot of cars drove by, but only a few people were on foot. A woman with a baby stroller stopped briefly and looked into the box.

teacher
expression

And then she looked at us like a teacher, and said what we were doing was **cruel to the animals,** because the poor rabbits didn't have enough room in the box.

"That's why we're selling them," I said, and held up a particularly cute rabbit. "So that they'll find a better home."

But she didn't buy **one**, even so.

 Cheyenne grinned at me. "What hops across the field smoking?"

I had no idea, and then she yelled, "A **burnny** rabbit!"

I almost choked, I was laughing so hard, but Chanelle kept shouting:

Huh? Why a burnny rabbit? Tell me!

After awhile, the whole thing wasn't any fun anymore. 😕 Maybe the rabbits were just too expensive. So I suggested we sell them for **five dollars.**

Cheyenne and Chanelle griped, but after half an hour they finally said **yes.**

Rabbits $~~10~~ 5

magic
recorder
$50

Beautiful,
cheap rabbits!
On **special today!**

Then a weird old guy with whiskers came along and looked in the box.

scratch

WHISKERS

FUNNY SMELL

Buy 'n Save

SAVE

Even Cheyenne didn't have anything to say.

Then he wanted to give us twenty dollars—for all of the rabbits together! We just shook our heads no, but Chanelle, yelled "Yes," really loud.

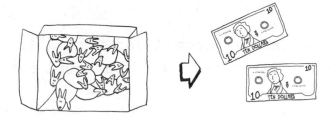

TWenty Dollars Was Way too little!

"**Two hundred** dollars," Cheyenne said, really bravely.

Then the man waved his arms around and ranted and raved at us and said he could buy a roasted rabbit for **three dollars** at the Buy 'n Save, already cut up.

And then, luckily, he went away, still ranting and raving and waving his arms around.

Cheyenne and I looked at each other, horrified.
He wanted to eat our rabbits!
No Way!

Each of us picked up a rabbit and stroked it.
They were so sweet and fluffy! You can't eat
something that cute!

Then we wrote **three dollars** on the sign. And
later, right before I had to go home, **one dollar.**

But **no one** bought a
rabbit, not even one.

Then a bicycle sailed around the corner and
on it sat Bernadette Bester. She was wearing
riding boots and a riding helmet. She looked
totally *ridiculous*.

riding
helmet

riding boots

I asked myself what she was doing here, where there are only apartment buildings, with nothing chic in sight. But then I remembered that there was a riding stable nearby.

trot

Bernadette stopped when she saw us. And gave us a snooty grin.

So, you're selling your dolls and picture books?

No, we're selling our riding helmets, because they make you look completely **crazy**.

Hee-hee-hee

I had to laugh out loud at that, especially when Bernadette gave us a **TOTALLY TOXIC** look from under her helmet.

Nevertheless, she came over to us and looked in the box.

snooty -->

And then she raised her eyebrows. So stuck-up.

"Oh, good grief," she muttered. "I could have guessed it."

"Oh, green goop," I muttered back at her. "I could have guessed your riding helmet would make you look like a **Gorilla with a perm.**"

That made Cheyenne giggle and Chanelle burst out laughing.

"You're all just too childish," Bernadette said, and started to get back on her bike.

But right at that moment Cheyenne jumped up to pat her on her back and say that we were just joking.

When Bernadette turned around to her, I saw that Cheyenne had stuck one of Chanelle's stickers on the back of her t-shirt.

And lhe sticker said:

I looked at Cheyenne and Cheyenne looked at me and then we both looked away, or else we probably would have died laughing.

Chanelle yelled, "What does that say?" but I quickly put my hand over her mouth.

hmmmmpff

Then Bernadette saw my recorder. "Well, it's probably a good thing that you're selling that," she said, **all stuck up.** "As miserably as you play! I've been taking violin lessons since I was four, and my violin teacher says that I have a lot of talent."

So I picked up my recorder and blew into it. Bernadette put her hands over her ears and stumbled backward.

But I kept playing.

And then something really **STRANGE** happened.

Namely, the cardboard box with the bunny rabbits burst open. And all of the rabbits scampered off, heading right for Bernadette.

Two hundred rabbits, booyah!

Bernadette turned and ran. She grabbed her bike, jumped on it, and pedaled off as fast as she could.

With the sticker on her back glowing bright yellow, like the yellow of a stoplight. --→

And all of the rabbits hopped along right behind her!

Cheyenne and I were laughing so hard we couldn't even run after the rabbits to catch them.

Ha! Ha! Ha!

I almost got a STOMACHACHE from laughing.

Only Chanelle screamed, and went running down the street, but there wasn't a rabbit in sight.

scream!

Except for **Scrappy**, of course, who wasn't so fast and was limping.

Then a bus came along and I had to save him.

Cheyenne wanted to help Chanelle, but every time we looked at each other we started laughing so hard she couldn't move. 😊

So unfortunately, we couldn't catch **any of the rabbits**, except for **Scrappy**.

At some point it was time for me to go home. Cheyenne said I should take **Scrappy** with me, but I didn't want to.

Even though I somehow had grown very fond of him, the way he was laying on the grass so peacefully, chewing on a dandelion.

But I wouldn't be able keep him anyway.

Then Cheyenne picked him up and stroked him and said that he could stay with her and Chanelle.

And then they would have **one rabbit**, at least, now that all the others had run off.

So I picked up my backpack and my recorder
and set off. There was a mailbox on the
corner of Main Street.

The recorder fit perfectly into the slot.

SATURDAY, AUGUST 27

Yippie! The Weekend!
Two whole days without
Ginny Crabbert and
Bernadette Bester!

Mrs. Crabbert

Bernadette

Today a funny noise woke me up. Kind of
like a **hissing** sound.

When I looked out the
window I saw Dad. ·····················>
He was standing on the
terrace with a **flame-thrower**,
torching the weeds that
were growing out of the
cracks.

torched
weeDs

hiss

flame-
thrower

Typical Dad!

I'm <u>not</u> allowed to have an MP3 player because he says that the **radiation** → will destroy my brain.

But then he's always buying the greatest things for himself!

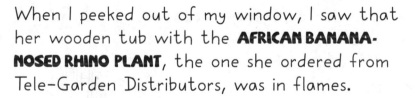

zzzzz I lay back down and fell asleep.

A little later, I woke up to Mom's screams.

Scream!

When I peeked out of my window, I saw that her wooden tub with the **AFRICAN BANANA-NOSED RHINO PLANT**, the one she ordered from Tele-Garden Distributors, was in flames.

click

Jacob and Simon were skipping around it like **Rumpelstiltskin** around a campfire, totally excited. ⇨

The next time 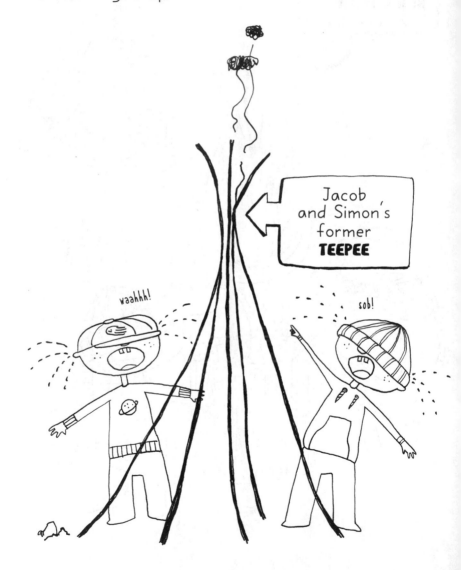 I was woken up,
it was due to the twins' howling.
That was because their **TEEPEE**
was burning down.
So then I got up.

Jacob
and Simon's
former
TEEPEE

waahhh!

sob!

By the time the mail came, I was already dressed and eating breakfast.
I usually don't get any mail, but this time there was something for me.

I could tell that when Mom came stomping in that the news **wasn't good.**

It was the recorder!

Mom slammed it down on the table in front of me so hard that the Choco Balls almost jumped out of my bowl at me. Then she demanded an explanation.

But I was as puzzled as she was, honest! And I found it a little **creepy** as well, because it couldn't really have happened. That the recorder had returned to me even though I hadn't written an address on it.

That afternoon, Cheyenne rang our doorbell and asked if I wanted to go to the county fair with her.

Of course I did! The county fair is the best thing there is, it's just too bad that it comes only twice a year.

Mom gave me ten dollars, and off we went.

Ten dollars is totally way too little for a **county fair**, because everything is so expensive. But luckily Cheyenne had **fifty** dollars with her.

I asked her where she got the money, and she said from her mother. **But I didn't believe that!** Cheyenne's mother isn't as stingy as mine. Still fifty dollars didn't sound right to me. Then Cheyenne said that her mother didn't exactly give her the money directly, but her purse was lying around open on the kitchen table.

> *Go ahead,*
> *take the money!*

"And if that's not what I would call, *'Go ahead, take the money!'* then I don't know what is," Cheyenne said.

I got a really **queasy** feeling when she said that. Because I know that's **definitely not** what my parents would call *Go ahead, take the money.*

But then I decided to be **happy** about it, because we had so much money and could go to the **county fair**.

It was totally packed with people, because it was Saturday, and it was crazy loud, and it smelled great.

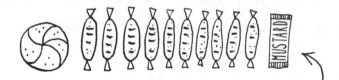

First off, Cheyenne bought herself **ten little sausages**, but I didn't, because I was still full from lunch.

We are here.

Then we took a ride on

Afterwards we felt totally **YUCKY**. Cheyenne even barfed up her ten little sausages.

And then she wanted to complain to the people who ran  because they let us on even though we're not twelve yet. "They have to give us our money back!" she said. "And the money for the sausages, too." But then she didn't do that, after all.

Instead, we tried drawing tickets. | TICKET |
We always draw tickets when we go to the
county fair, but usually all we ever win is rubber
bats  or wax teeth.
We've never once won anything cool.

But this time we did! On my first draw I picked
the **BIG PRIZE!** It was a giant panda, almost as
big as me! I've always wanted one.

Cheyenne was a bit ANNOYED.
First, the thing with the sausages,
and then I win the **BIG PRIZE**.

As we were walking around, everybody
was looking at us with ENVY because
I was holding a **giant panda**. Or more precisely:
I was carrying it in both arms.
Because it was **so big** that I couldn't
carry it in one arm.

Then we both ate an **ice cream cone.** At least I tried to. But I couldn't, because I didn't have a hand free. Cheyenne held out my cone to me so that I could lick the ice cream, but then she had to eat most of it herself to keep it from dripping.

And then my arms started hurting. I got the feeling that they were growing longer and longer.

 I was sweating, because the **Panda** was so thick and warm.

So I told Cheyenne that I really needed to sit down somewhere <u>right away</u>.

groan... ...

Cheyenne had the **genius idea** that we should go sit down in the **roller coaster**.

I thought that sounded good, so we went over to the roller coaster and bought tickets.

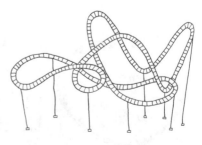

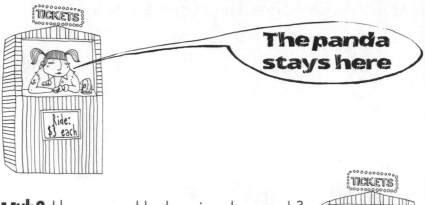

Huh? How was that going to work? Who was going to watch him? He couldn't just sit around somewhere all by himself—he'd get **stolen!**

So then the lady said I'd have to pay full price for him because he would take up a whole seat. That would mean it would cost six dollars for the two of us. 🙁 And I didn't have that much money left.

But Cheyenne was totally sweet and paid for all the tickets.

Squeal!

this way down

She even bought a whole lot of tickets at once because, she said, the ride goes by so fast. And then we all sat next to each other, Cheyenne and I on the outside and **Panda** in the middle, and we took **four rides** on the roller coaster. Whenever it headed down, we all raised our arms and screamed.

hee-hee-hee

It was almost like flying. When we got off, our hair was completley messy, and only **Panda** looked normal.

After that, Cheyenne **BRAIN BLASTER** wanted to ride the but I sat down on a bench with **Panda** and waited for her. The sun was shining, the crowd was noisy, and very **county fair-ish,** and everyone grinned when they saw me and **Panda.**

It smelled good, too, like roasted almonds.

I was slowly getting hungry.

When Cheyenne got off the **BRAIN BLASTER** she bought some roasted almonds. ⟶ And candy canes and popsicles and bracelets that we could nibble on and a baby bottle filled with sprinkles and a bag of waffle bits, and then we went home.

Cheyenne fed me roasted almonds, and when **Panda** got too heavy for me she carried him. Then it was my turn to stuff waffle bits and

sprinkles in her mouth, which made her laugh.

Unfortunately, when she laughed she slobbered on **Panda** a little. But that only made us laugh harder.

Cheyenne walked me to my house. Then she gave me the rest of the almonds. And a bracelet and a baby bottle with sprinkles.

I rang the **bell,** *Ding* and when Dad opened the door I showed him **Panda.**

And first, of course, he had to say a bunch of rude things. Like the garbage would be picked up on Monday, and so on. But I didn't care.

Because, I went to the twins' room and showed them **Panda,** so that they would get **jealous.** And boy, were they **jealous!**

Though Simon said that a panda was totally lame and monkeys were a hundred times cooler. And Jacob said that a seam had burst on **Panda's** rear end and **A LONG PIECE OF...SOMETHING** was coming out.

So I took a look, and a seam really had burst. But it was some kind of scratchy stuffing that was spilling out back there. I showed **Panda** to Mom, and she promised to sew him up when she had time.

Later, I had to practice the recorder. 😐

man, I'm so sick and tired of practicing the recorder!

And to make matters worse, the **weirdest** things happen when I play. 😵

I took **Panda** to my room and put him on the bed with Helga and the rest of my stuffed animals.

Helga is a horned sheep, I got her when I was really little. She has these funny horns sewn to her head. Dad said that she was wearing a Viking helmet and that her name was Helga, the Warrior Sheep.

Only later did I realize that she was called Helga only because Dad said so. I actually would have liked to give her a **pretty** sheep's name, like

⤷ (Missy) or (Daisy) ✳ ✳

Both Helga and **Panda** are very big. There's not much room left for me on the bed.

I left my bedroom door open. So that everyone could enjoy the music. Then I grabbed my recorder and blew into it.

A **terrible noise** came out. And a little bit of **spit.**

And then something happened again!

Panda grabbed both Helga and my Stuffed Lamb Vulture, from the bird sanctuary.

baa!

And then he pressed them against both ears. But because Helga is a warrior sheep, she defended herself and started baa-ing.

And then **Panda** threw Helga onto the bed and held Lumpy the Dog against his ear instead.

Panda's Arm

yikes!

I stopped playing right away. I stared at my animals, but they were normal stuffed toys again.

And then it became clear to me: **The recorDer haD to Go!!!** Otherwise, more **very baD** things were going to happen. ☹

I put it in my closet, way back under my ski socks, and locked the door.

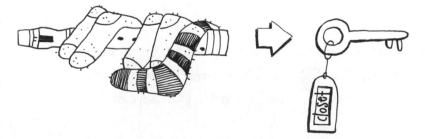

SUNDAY, AUGUST 28

Today I was at Cheyenne's, and gave her **Panda**. Which made her totally happy.

In her and Chanelle's room it doesn't matter if they add a **Giant Panda** to the mix. There are so many things in there already that you can't even see the floor.

Cheyenne wanted to give me a candy cane or a popsicle to thank me, but she and Chanelle had eaten all of them already.

MONDAY, AUGUST 29

Today Mrs. Crabbert came up with another annoying assignment. We were supposed to describe an animal, and guess which animal it was?

The **Panda!** Luckily, I'm an expert on pandas!

I wrote that pandas <u>really don't like</u> listening to recorder music.

And I also shared that it's possible that pandas might burst open at their rear end.

> **Do it over!**

psh!

But Mrs. Crabbert doesn't know much about pandas. She just made an angry psshing sound and told me I had to take it home and do it over.

UNFAIR!

Bernadette laughed herself silly, **the biG snob.** I think she doesn't like me very much lately. I may have accidentally called her **BernaDork**.

Bernadork

It's not so bad that Bernadette doesn't like me. I don't like her, either. It's just that today she formed a girls gang and all of the girls in our class want to join. Only Cheyenne and I are left out.

So maybe we'll just form our own gang, Cheyenne said at recess. **Good idea!**

maybe:

TOO COOL FOR SCHOOL

or

THE WILD RABBITS

WR

or

The 2 secret BLOODSISTERS

THE WILD RABBITS

WEDNESDAY, AUGUST 31

Cheyenne is really **lucky!**
Because she has:

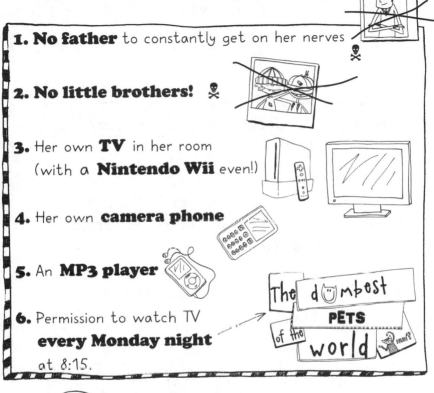

1. No father to constantly get on her nerves ☠

2. No little brothers! ☠

3. Her own **TV** in her room
   (with a **Nintendo Wii** even!)

4. Her own **camera phone**

5. An **MP3 player**

6. Permission to watch TV
   every Monday night
   at 8:15.

Guess where I am at 8:15
every Monday night! **In
beD, of course!** Even
though I'd like to see
at least just
once!

The d☺mbest PETS of the world

But Mom always says that I need my sleep, and Dad says  that it's a junky program and we  don't watch things like that.

It's totally annoyinG that parents get to decide on things like that!

And besides, it's not true that it's junky. Cheyenne always tells me about it, and it sounds like **total fun**!

Funny things happen to animals. That's why people film them!

And then they send it in to the TV channel, and if it's shown on TV, they get 100 dollars.

One hundred dollars! I could use that kind of money. For my pet, of course. 😄

But unfortunately we don't have a camera at home, nor a cell phone with a camera.

That's Dad's fault. He is stuck, technologically speaking, in the ⇦ **STONE AGE.**

He still believes that a VCR is something **GREAT.**

So I asked Cheyenne if we could make a **funny** animal video together.

Cheyenne and Lotta, the cool animal filmmakers

In the afternoon, after we had done our homework, we took off.

Cheyenne had her camera phone with her, because you can film with it. I had my recorder with me because I'm still looking for a way to get rid of it somewhere.

At first we only ran around outside Cheyenne's building, where the garbage bins are.

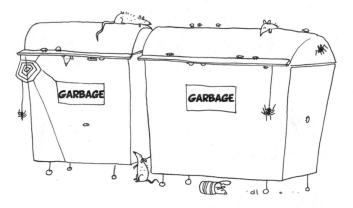

Mostly because Cheyenne said that sometimes she sees rats there. But all I saw were **DISGUSTING** spiders and bugs, and anyway, I don't find rats all that funny.

I guess I don't find all animals cool, just most of them.

But there are some animals that I'd **never, ever Want in my life** as a pet. Namely:

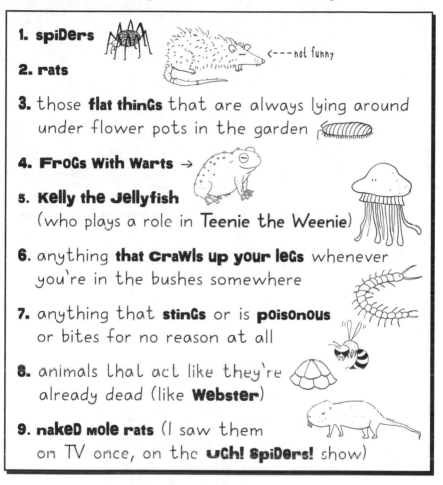

1. spiDers

2. rats

<----not funny

3. those **flat thinGs** that are always lying around under flower pots in the garden

4. FroGs With Warts →

5. Kelly the Jellyfish
(who plays a role in **Teenie the Weenie**)

6. anything **that CraWls up your leGs** whenever you're in the bushes somewhere

7. anything that **stinGs** or is **poisonOus** or bites for no reason at all

8. animals that act like they're already dead (like **Webster**)

9. nakeD mole rats (I saw them on TV once, on the **uCh! SpiDers!** show)

After that we went to the new housing development, where we ran into a **cat**. Cheyenne wanted to go after her, because she had a **funnY** plan in mind.

But the cat only strolled around. Boring. At one
house there was a garage with the door open
and no car inside, and she walked in. And from
there she walked through a cat door right into
the house.

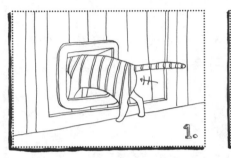

That wasn't good.

We just stood there and didn't know what
to do. "Where does the cat live?" Cheyenne
asked me.

Huh? What did that mean?
But then she started giggling.
"In the cathouse!" Ha! Ha! Ha! Ha! Ha!

I had to laugh. Then Cheyenne said I should
crawl through the **Cat Door.** I stopped
laughing at that. "Why me?" I asked.

shorter

wider

thinner

"It's clear, man," she said. "You're much smaller and thinner than me, because you only just turned ten. I couldn't fit through there."

And she was right, of course. So I started crawling through. But then I couldn't fit through the flap, and I **got stuck.** Right about where my stomach is.

At first I was **afraid** that the people who lived here would come back and see me. Because they certainly wouldn't think it was a good thing to find me stuck in their cat door.

Hello!

But then I became totally **afraid** that I wouldn't be able to get out.

So I **screamed.** Luckily, Cheyenne was there and pulled me out by my legs. But only after I'd been screaming for a pretty long time. And I kept screaming, because it **hurt** when Cheyenne was pulling me out.

The flap was so small that it was scraping everything—my stomach, my ribs, my arms.

And I didn't find it funny at all that once I finally was outside, Cheyenne was still laughing. ☹

But then she showed me her phone. She had filmed me, stuck in the flap, kicking and screaming.

kicking

And then she said that maybe we should submit it to because it was **so funny.**

The dumbest PETS of the world

Ha! Ha!

ow!

I started to laugh, too, though my ribs still felt a **little broken.**

When we'd finished laughing we kept walking until we had left the new housing development. The whole time we talked about what we wanted to buy with our fifty dollars.

Cheyenne said that she wanted to buy a **robot-dinosaur** with remote control.

Or a **waveboard.**

Along the way, we passed a meat market. Cheyenne was hungry and wanted to buy two sausages. She asked if I wanted one, too, but I didn't. I went in with her anyway.

And then I noticed what a **great opportunity** this was! I took the recorder out of my backpack, and then stood right next to the display window in front, the one with all the meat.

When the lady behind the counter wasn't looking, I quickly stuck the recorder between a couple of homemade sausages. ☺

Cheyenne paid for the sausages and we left the shop. Cheyenne wanted to eat them both right away, but when she opened the bag, there was only **one** sausage inside.

And a recorder.

THURSDAY, SEPTEMBER 1

Today, we really wanted to get down to filming our funny pet video!

So we reviewed which animals we would choose. I immediately thought of **Polly.** →

Then on second thought, that didn't seem like such a good idea. 😐

Mrs. Lopez's parrot --→ would be great, but I just didn't see it happening. So Cheyenne said she'd ring her doorbell and ask.

I thought that was totally brave, especially since Cheyenne doesn't even know Mrs. Lopez.

I hid behind a garbage can so Mrs. Lopez wouldn't see me when she looked out of the door. She saw me anyway; she looked out of an upstairs window. And of course she didn't let Polly out. Instead she gave Cheyenne WHAT FOR.

yell
fuss
grumble

Her parrot, Hannibal, was screeching in the
SCREECH! background. He screeched like he was getting murdered. You have to feel sorry for the poor thing, it must really hurt his nymph glands, the way he's always screaming.

"Man, what a **WeirDo,**" Cheyenne said when she came back. And she used a lot of other words, some of which I'd never heard before.

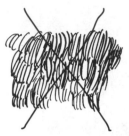

Okay, so Polly won't get to be on television and be famous! There are plenty of dogs running around in the park that we can film.

We saw two dogs right away when we got there. And they were **pugs.** They looked totally cute. And **funny.** Just right for our pet video!

"Hey, he's the *ONE*," Cheyenne whispered to me. "I think he's totally sweet!" I asked her which one she meant. Because one was **black** and the other one white.

But Cheyenne wasn't talking about the dogs. She meant the boy who was walking them. And the boy was **Kevin**, Bernadette's brother.

Bernadette, Bernadork

Sister of

Cheyenne waved to him, but he didn't see her because he was busy with the pugs.

They had run away. "Pompey! Pugsley! Heel!" he cried, but Pompey and Pugsley <u>didn't</u> obey. They came running right at us. And then they both jumped up on Cheyenne, twirling around and whimpering. As if they were just so happy.

gruntgruntgrunt
whimperwhimper

I was a **little jealous** that they were jumping up on Cheyenne and not on me. Cheyenne petted them and they got even more excited, and were so funny the way they snuffled. They really were cute!

Kevin came running across
the grass with their leash,
but then someone else arrived:
(**a shaggy dog**) with short
little legs. He also jumped up
on Cheyenne and snapped at
her dress a little.
That's when she hopped
back a few steps.

But then when a
(poodle with a poodle cut)
also came shooting like
a rocket through the
flowerbeds, I wasn't
a bit jealous anymore.

Cheyenne turned
around and ran.

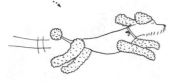

In the meantime, Kevin came over to where I was, looking not half as sweet as his pugs. **Seriously.** His hair was a little long and he had a totally angry expression on his face.

long hair

Pompey! Heel!

angry face

Then he took off after them and so did I. We sprinted behind Cheyenne and the dogs. And then a giant schnauzer raced by us. He was chasing after Cheyenne, too, and barking and looking very happy, the giant schnauzer.

woof woof

Cheyenne had reached the pond and couldn't go any further. The dogs were jumping all over her, whimpering and howling and barking and slobbering.

Then, when a German shepherd also appeared through the bushes, Cheyenne jumped into the pond. The dogs were very happy about this and dove in headlong after her.

"Help! I can't swim!" she cried, gurgling and sinking in the water.

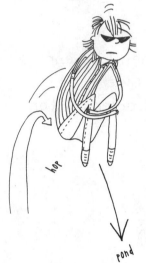

So Kevin had to save her. He looked pretty ANNOYED when he jumped into the pond in his chic shirt.

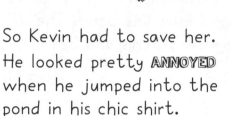

And even more annoyed when he noticed that the water wasn't even that deep, and that Cheyenne could have stood up in it.

But he carried her out anyway.
Cheyenne thought that was pretty cool.
She told him that he had saved her life and
that she would go to the movies with him as a
thank you. But he just snarled, "No thanks!"

And then they just stood there, looking at all
of the dogs swimming around in the water.

Every once in a while Kevin
would call Pompey and Pugsley,
but mostly he just stood there,
quietly dripping.

Pompey!
Pugsley!

Then suddenly, Cheyenne looked **TOTALLY
SCARED** as she reached into the big pocket in
her dress.

SHOCK!

squish

My cell!

But luckily, her cell wasn't in her
pocket. Only a wet paper bag from
Burger Paradise. Along with half
of a soaking Double Whopler.

yuck

slap!

"Oh, now I get why all the dogs were after me," she said, beaming.

squish

"Because this smelled so good." And then she took a bite of the Double Whopper. Even though it looked pretty squishy.

We didn't do any filming after that. And anyway, Cheyenne had left her phone at home.

Typical Cheyenne: cell phone sitting next to one of her dolls in a toy car.

We no longer wanted to make any funny pet videos. It hadn't been as much fun as we thought it would be.
Instead, I got the idea that maybe we could make a **funny** film about Webster while playing my **recorder.** ⟶

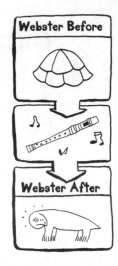

And then I told Cheyenne that my recorder wasn't normal. That it's the **recorder** that's responsible when **strange** things happen.

"I can do a funny thing, too," Cheyenne said. "I can wiggle my ears. Watch this!"

I watched while she made **a whole lot of faces.**
But her ears did **not** wiggle when she did.

FRIDAY, SEPTEMBER 2

So, now that we aren't going to make funny pet movies I don't want a pet anymore. For some reason, I've had it with animals.
I'd rather have a **camera phone** just like Cheyenne's.

Just to be sure, I told this to Dad. Christmas is in three months, after all.

But you can't talk to Dad about stuff like that! Right away he had to explain to me how he and his brother Henry phoned each other when they were kids...with **telephones they made out of yogurt cups** connected with a string.

And then they stood in a field and Henry shouted, "Hello, Robert," and Dad answered back, "Hello, Henry."

HOW Dorky!

Of course Jacob and Simon found it just fascinating, and immediately started making a yogurt cup telephone.

But Jacob's cup still had a little **raspberry yogurt** inside, so he couldn't hear so good through it. "You smelly monkey fart!" he shouted into it, and a little yogurt dripped out of his ear.

You super kooky numbskull!

All of our neighbors could hear their conversation, even without yogurt cup telephones.

*T*hen that evening, once the boys were asleep, Barney chatted on the phone for a while with Simon. Barney has such nice long arms that it was easy to tuck a yogurt cup telephone under one of them. And the cord was so long that I could sit in the bathroom across the hall and talk into the other cup.

Me with a yogurt cup

Barney with the other one

Your final hour has struck, for I am the monkey of death! Ho ho ho!

It worked super great.
Simon woke up, screaming
bloody murder.

WAAAAAAH

Even though I immediately went to my room
and got in bed, I got in big trouble, of course.
UNFAIR!

bling

zzzzz

And the whole **riDiculous** yogurt cup
telephone thing hadn't even been my idea!

SUNDAY, SEPTEMBER 4

whisper

Mom's secret expression

There was some kind of secret thing going on today. This morning Mom was on the phone with somebody and then she had a long talk with Dad in the kitchen and then she made another phone call.

When I asked what was going on, she just got a secret expression on her face. Like there was going to be a surprise soon.

Then I got very antsy. Did it perhaps have something to do with a camera phone?

Later, I wanted to go over to Cheyenne's, but Dad said that I should stay home, because we were waiting for something. And that it was something I would find **really fantastic.** Which—of course—made me even more excited. **This was worse than waiting for Christmas!**

I didn't know what to do, so I checked what the boys were up to.
Jacob and Simon were in the garden, playing **APES IN SPACE** with Barney and Fishy.
Fishy, the flat flounder, was the **SPACEFISH ENTERPRISE.**

Because I had nothing better to do, I went to get Helga, the galactic super-sheep. And then together they all saved humanity. And the rest of the universe, too.

After that, I waited some more. PHOOEY, that went on for a long time. My nerves were totally shot, and then finally the doorbell rang. "Ring!"

⇨ So naturally I jumped up and ran for the door. At least that's what I wanted to do, but then something came between me and it.

stumble

I had stumbled over Webster, who was lying in the middle of the living room. (I'll write more about Webster later. I don't have the time right now!!!) So Mom got to the door first.

Somebody screamed. As if he were being murdered. **SCREECH!** And then Mom was walking toward me. With a huge cage in her arms.

I thought I was seeing things. It was **Hannibal**, Mrs. Lopez's parrot. The one with the nymph problem.

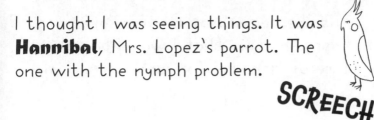

SCREECH

Then he was screeching again, as loud as the brakes of two trains trying not to collide. The animal must, I think, be really very sick.

And behind Mom was a woman I didn't know. She was telling Mom that her mother would have to stay in the hospital for at least three weeks.

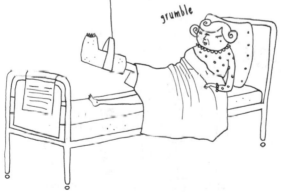

grumble

"Fractured ankle, torn ligament...well, Mother won't be playing tennis again any time soon," she was saying.

gulp!

And she beamed at me and said how happy she was that I would be taking care of Hannibal for such a long time.

Then Mom beamed at me and said that now I could show how I could take responsibility for a pet.

SCREECH!

Dad didn't beam, and said that if the creature was going to make that much noise, he would have to stay in my room the whole time.

SCREECH!

I froze in shock, and just
looked at Hannibal.

Shock!

Who looked back at me quite sweetly and
almost smiled a bit with his red cheeks. So I
stuck a finger in his cage, because I thought
that would be the best way for him to get
used to me.

red cheeks

And then Hannibal took **a giant bite** out
of me. There was a big hole in my finger.
Then he screeched again, like someone
was being murdered. **SCREECH!**

I think I'll take him to the vet right away
tomorrow morning. Maybe to have his nymphs
removed.

SCREECH!

Bernadette Bester

↰ brother of

Kevin Bester

The coolest boy at school (according to Cheyenne)

From my class → is pretty rich, I think

animals

HANNIBAL

bird of→

Polly and Mrs. Lopez

Our neighbor and her dog (sweet!)

pesky brothers ↘

Jacob and Simon Petermann

Twins

always looking sternly over her glasses

our class teacher →

Mrs. Crabbert